MW00768192

Krick

A Pie for Thanksgiving

To: Westley
+
Grant

"Best Wishes"

Paul Evans
11-7-98

A Pie for Thanksgiving

by

Paul Evans

Illustrated by

Jane Lenoir

Ozark Publishing, Inc.
P.O. Box 228
Prairie Grove, AR 72753

Library of Congress cataloging-in-publication data

Evans, Paul, 1950-
    A pie for Thanksgiving / by Paul Evans ;
illustrated by Jane Lenoir.
        p.   cm.
    Summary: The arrival of a new family of rabbits
in the village causes one of Mrs. Cottontail's
Thanksgiving pies to disappear but provides the oppor-
tunity for everyone to show forgiveness and generosity.
    ISBN 1-56763-265-3 (cloth : alk. paper). — ISBN
1-56763-266-1(pbk. : alk. paper)
    [1. Rabbits--Fiction. 2. Thanksgiving
Day—Fiction. 3. Forgiveness—Fiction.] I. Title.
PZ7.E89224Pi 1997
[E]—dc20   96-27280
                                                    CIP
                                                     AC

Copyright © 1997 by Paul Evans
All rights reserved

Printed in the United States of America

Inspired by
my love of books and a desire to
create my own style of writing.

Dedicated to
my family, whom I love dearly.

Foreword

Each year Mrs. Cottontail baked Thanksgiving pies for her friends and neighbors. A new family of rabbits moved into the village, and one of the children took one of Mrs. Cottontail's carrot pies. Seeing how poor the new family was, Mrs. Cottontail and her friends forgave them. On Thanksgiving Day, all the rabbits in the village carried gifts to the new family. Mrs. Cottontail baked them a pie, and they all sat down to Thanksgiving dinner.

A Pie for Thanksgiving

It was late autumn, the day before Thanksgiving, the time for giving thanks and for being close to loved ones as the year drew to an end.

Mrs. Cottontail, a sweet little old rabbit, worked hurriedly in the kitchen of her house, baking Thanksgiving pies. Each year at Thanksgiving, she baked carrot pies for all her friends to show them how much she loved them and to thank them for being nice to her.

The day was such a warm and beautiful one that she decided to place the pies on the windowsill in her kitchen to cool in the gentle

breeze before she delivered them to her friends. While the pies were cooling, she decided to make herself a pot of tea.

Mrs. Cottontail placed the kettle on the stove to heat. She turned to check on her pies once more. To her surprise, she saw a strange rabbit running away with one of her pies. She yelled at him, but he kept on running until he was out of sight.

Mrs. Cottontail wept softly, because she had baked only enough pies for her friends. She did not know why that boy would want to steal one of them. It was getting late, and she did

not have time to bake another one.

I'll just have to explain to the last one on my list what happend to that pie, she thought.

She made her tea and then drank it before carefully packing the remaining pies into a basket. She then hurried off to deliver them.

Along the way, Mrs. Cottontail told everyone what had happened, and each one thought it was a mean thing that happened to her.

Finally, all the pies were delivered, and she had one more rabbit on her list who would not

receive a pie for Thanksgiving. That rabbit was Mr. Jumping Jack, the oldest and wisest of all the rabbits in the village. When Mrs. Cottontail arrived at his house, she told him what had happened.

He said, "Oh, Mrs. Cottontail, I know who stole your pie. Just a little while ago, I was down in the briar patch picking berries. A small rabbit came running by, and he was carrying a pie."

Mr. Jumping Jack told her that a new family had moved into the village a couple of days before. They lived just across

the field at the edge of the woods.

The two of them decided to go over to visit the new family and to see if the rabbit who had stolen Mrs. Cottontail's pie lived with them. They walked across the field to the edge of the woods and finally came to a little mushroom-shaped cottage.

Mrs. Cottontail knocked on the door. The door opened to a dark and empty house. A dirty-faced little girl rabbit stood inside the doorway. Mrs. Cottontail asked her if her mother or father were home.

She said, "There is no one

here but my mother and my
brother. I don't have a father.
He went away and left us all
alone."

A thin little mother rabbit
appeared in the doorway behind
her daughter. In the background
was her son, and he was eating a
piece of the pie.

Mrs. Cottontail told the
mother rabbit the story about how
she always baked Thanksgiving
pies for all her friends and
neighbors. She said, "I believe
your son has taken the one that I
was going to give to Mr. Jumping
Jack."

The mother rabbit began to

weep. She said that she was sorry that her son had stolen the pie. "We were hungry and did not know where else to find food." She promised Mrs. Cottontail that someday she would repay her for the pie.

Seeing how poor those rabbits were made Mr. Jumping Jack and Mrs. Cottontail feel very sad. They told the mother rabbit that it was all right; it was plain to see that the new family had no food to eat.

"We can see that you needed the pie; we don't mind that you ate it," Mrs. Cottontail explained. They said goodbye and left.

Early the next morning, which was Thanksgiving Day, all the rabbits of the village gathered together to give thanks as they usually did on Thanksgiving Day, but that day was different. Instead of their customary activities, they collected food, clothing, and all sorts of odds and ends to give to the new family in the village. They loaded up their baskets and carts and started toward the home of the poor family.

When they arrived, they found the little mother rabbit and her two children weeping openly. They apparently thought the

other rabbits of the village had come to drive them away because they had stolen the pie to fill their empty stomachs. To their surprise, the villagers stopped and began to unload all the stuff that they had packed, then they carried it to the doorway of the little house. Upon seeing that, the tears of sadness in their eyes became tears of joy, because it was the first time that anyone had been that nice to them.

The village rabbits unloaded the food and gifts and carried them into the house. The son who had stolen the pie worked extra hard, because he still felt

sad and ashamed for taking the pie without asking for it. Soon everything was unloaded, and everyone wondered what had happened to Mrs. Cottontail. She still had not arrived.

Finally she came hurriedly down the trail. It was the first time anyone had seen her move that fast.

She arrived, completely out of breath. She told them that she had thought about the family not having a pie for Thanksgiving and decided to bake one for them.

She called to the little boy
rabbit and said, "This is a pie for
Thanksgiving for you and your
family." She told him that she
would bake a pie for them, as
she did for all of her friends

each year, if he promised to help her deliver them.

He said, "Yes, Mrs. Cottontail, I will be glad to help you deliver your pies for Thanksgiving each year."

His mother said that she would help with the baking.

His little sister said, "Me, too. I'll help with the baking, Mrs. Cottontail."

They all sat down to have dinner and gave thanks with the new family of the village.